MAX

and the

WON'T GO TO BED

SHOW

Mark Sperring and Sarah Warburton

HarperCollins *Children's Books*

Ladies and gentlemen! Boys and girls!
Roll up, roll up, for the
GREATEST SHOW ON EARTH!

Tonight for your entertainment and
delight we proudly present, from all
the way behind the curtain,
the world's youngest magician.
Please put your hands together for...

MAX THE MAGNIFICENT!

Tonight we will see his world famous
and death-defying

**PUTTING OFF BEDTIME FOR
AS LONG AS POSSIBLE SHOW!**

For his first trick, Max the Magnificent
will make one cup of milk and one whole
cookie disappear before our very eyes...

v...e...r...y s...l...o...w...l...y...

A ... b ... r ... a ... c ... a ... d ... a ... b ... r ... a!

Now we must ask the audience to remain calm. For his second trick, Max will

TAME THE MOST SAVAGE OF BEASTS.

The savage beast's name is Brian.
(Brian likes walks in the park,
tickles behind the ears and carrying
round old slippers in his mouth.)

That's not sit!

"Fetch, savage beast, fetch!"

YUK!

That's not fetch!

It's a big, slurpy good night kiss and
that can only mean one thing...

BEDTIME!

Max the Magnificent is led up the stairs
of doom. Surely it can't be bedtime yet?
Max isn't even slightly tired!

Time for another trick...

...THE GREAT DISAPPEARING BOY TRICK!

Max, where are you?

Is he behind the chair,
ladies and gentlemen?

No, here he is in the bathroom cleaning his teeth!

What a GLitteRing extravaganza!

What a DAZZLing spectacle!

This CERTAINLY deserves a **BIG** round of applause!

And now prepare to be SHOCKED and AMAZED.
You are about to witness the seldom seen

FLOATING PYJAMA TRICK.

Max will cause his pyjamas to lift off the chair,
float across the room and, perhaps the most
difficult part of all, attempt to put them on.

Audience be warned, this trick can
take up to half an hour to perform...

Though luckily not tonight...

TA DA!

The show isn't over yet. There are still more thrills to be had...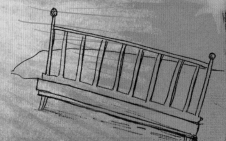

Max the Magnificent pulls a rabbit from under the bed.

BRAVO!

And a bear from out of the wardrobe.

HURRAH!

And his favourite stripy raccoon from out of the toy box.

ENCORE!

Next, as Max the Magnificent crawls
into bed he will attempt the impossible.

Ladies and gentlemen, boys and girls,
we strongly advise you

NEVER

to try this at home...

Max asks for ten – yes, tEN! – bedtime stories.

(His mum says she'll read two.)

Now we must dim the lights and ask for hush. Let's tiptoe out and leave our little magician in peace.

Thank you, ladies and gentlemen. Good night, boys and girls.

Max the Magnificent needs his sleep now. After all...

...who knows what tricks he'll pull tomorrow?

For Harry (Mágico Chico!) – MS
Ditto – SW

First published in hardback in Great Britain by HarperCollins Children's Books in 2013

First published in paperback in 2014

1 3 5 7 9 10 8 6 4 2

ISBN: 978-0-00-746838-6

HarperCollins Children's Books is a division of HarperCollins Publishers Ltd.

The author and illustrator assert the moral right to be identified as the author and illustrator of the work.

A CIP catalogue record for this title is available from the British Library.

Text copyright © Mark Sperring 2013. Illustrations copyright © Sarah Warburton 2013

Visit our website at: www.harpercollins.co.uk. Printed in China